THE CHILDREN OF CROW COVE SERIES

BY BODIL BREDSDORFF

The Crow-Girl

Eidi

Tink

Alek

Alek

The Children of Crow Cove Series

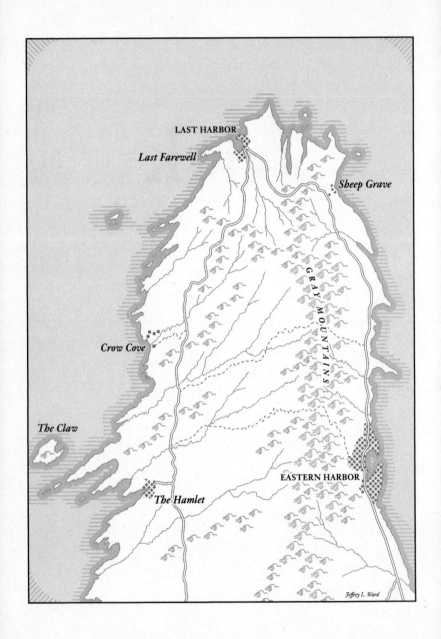

Alek

The Children of Crow Cove Series

BODIL BREDSDORFF

Translated from the Danish by
ELISABETH KALLICK DYSSEGAARD

Farrar Straus Giroux • New York

Farrar Straus Giroux Books for Young Readers
175 Fifth Avenue, New York 10010

Distributed in Canada by D&M Publishers, Inc.
Printed in the United States of America by RR Donnelley & Sons,
Harrisonburg, Virginia
First edition, 2012
1   3   5   7   9   10   8   6   4   2

mackids.com

Library of Congress Cataloging-in-Publication Data
Bredsdorff, Bodil.
    [Alek. English]
    Alek / Bodil Bredsdorff ; translated from the Danish by Elisabeth
Kallick Dyssegaard. — 1st ed.
        p.   cm. — (The children of Crow Cove series)
    Originally published in Danish under the title: Alek: børnene i kragevig 4.
    Summary: Leaving behind Crow Cove and Doup, the name he was called
there, Alek journeys to his heartbroken older brother's home in the fishing
village of Last Harbor, where Alek finds work at an inn and rescues a
beautiful foreigner whose parents were killed by ship wreckers.
    ISBN 978-0-374-31269-5 (hardcover)
    ISBN 978-0-374-12345-1 (e-book)
    [1. Conduct of life—Fiction.   2. Brothers—Fiction.   3. Taverns
(Inns)—Fiction.   4. Shipwrecks—Fiction.   5. Orphans—Fiction.]
I. Dyssegaard, Elisabeth Kallick.   II. Title.

PZ7.B74814Ale 2012
[Fic]—dc23

2011031670

Alek

The Children of Crow Cove Series

1

A mass of driftwood floated down the desolate shore. The waves pushed and shoved the ribs and staves and threw the wood toward land only to pull it out again.

The wood floated by a small cove with a few whitewashed houses and then farther along the stony beach. A split oar was thrown off course and all the way in to the water's edge, where it was seized and flung to higher ground beyond the reach of the waves.

* * *

The boy who had taken the oar from the sea dried his hand on his pants leg before he stuck it into his pocket again. The oar could lie there until a day when they collected driftwood. And they weren't doing that today.

They were searching, he and the young woman who walked next to him and the black dog that ran ahead of them.

They were searching for his little horse, which he had had as long as he could remember. Forever. It had eyes that looked black but were also clear as glass, brown like seaweed, and deep blue when you looked into them. And it had thick brown fur through which his hands had raked thousands of tracks, from the time they were small and hesitant to now when they were used to work and confident.

His little horse for which he had long been way too big.

He couldn't remember a day when he hadn't spoken to it, touched it, fed it, and groomed it—until it disappeared.

They had searched inland and up by the sheep,

along the stream, behind bushes and rocks. Soon there would be no place left to search.

"We need to go home," said the woman, "before it gets dark."

He knew it.

"Glennie!" she shouted, but the dog didn't come back.

They could hear her barking farther down the coast where she had hunted out a flock of gulls. The birds fled inland with hoarse screams, leaving behind a carcass between the rocks.

The gulls had pecked out the horse's eyes before they began picking the meat from the bones. The empty eye sockets saw nothing under the dark forelock, which the wind ruffled thoughtlessly.

The boy stomped his foot.

"Oh, Myna, why didn't it stay in its stall?" he exclaimed.

She walked over and stood next to him.

"Maybe it preferred to die out here by the sea."

"Dumb birds!"

"It doesn't feel anything, and gulls are always hungry. To them it is not your horse but just some meat, lying here rotting."

Glennie had walked around the dead animal and carefully sniffed it. Now the dog sat down next to Myna and began to whimper.

"Come on! There's nothing we can do," said Myna, and patted Glennie on the head.

But the boy continued to stand and stare. The dog grew quiet and lay down, resting her head on her front paws. The gulls had sent out a lone scout, who circled high above them. Glennie lay stock-still, following it with her eyes.

"In a couple of days, I'll go and collect the skull," said Myna, "when it has been picked clean. Then we can use it for Dark Night."

They usually had a candle stuck in a ram's skull as the light that would burn all of Dark Night while the year died, until Light Morning when the New Year was born.

He nodded and turned away from the horse and started the walk back to the small cove. Myna and Glennie followed.

* * *

The wind had subsided, and the sky was gray and heavy and pulled the light out of the world and made the rocks slippery. He had to take his hands out of his pockets to keep his balance.

In between the rocks were small, stony beaches where they could walk side by side.

"I remember the first time I saw you," said Myna. Her hoarse voice was low and mild. "I asked you what your name was and you said Doup."

Doup smiled. "And that was just because I wanted soup." He had been very small. Myna had come to their house when his father was out of his mind with grief after his mother died, and taken Doup away with her to Crow Cove. He had lived with her ever since, even after his father, Frid, and his brother, Ravnar, had come after him and made their home in Crow Cove, too.

"Look," said Myna, and pointed out to sea.

A school of porpoises came tumbling close to the shore. Their dark backs with low dorsal fins drew arcs in the water. Myna and Doup watched them until they disappeared.

*　*　*

It was almost dark when they got home. There was no light in the first house they came to, so they continued across the bridge and steered toward the faint glow from the house on the opposite bank of the stream.

When they stepped into Frid and Foula's parlor, the air was warm and close with food smells. Five people sat around the table. Frid got up and came to meet them. He nodded at Myna and looked at Doup. The boy dried a drop of water off his nose with the back of his hand.

"We found the little horse," said Myna. "It's dead."

"It was old," said Frid. "It was older than you," he said to Doup, and carefully placed a hand on his son's shoulder.

"Come and have something to eat before the food gets cold," said Foula.

Doup shook his head, pulled away and sat down on the settle. Myna sat down at the table.

"Why is it dead?" asked a chubby little boy with his mouth full of food.

"Go ahead and eat, Cam!" said Foula, his mother.

"I am," said the boy, and went on. "How could you tell that it was dead? Had it closed its eyes?"

"It didn't have eyes at all anymore," said Doup. "The gulls had pecked them out."

"When there aren't any eyes," asked Cam, "what is there then? What's behind them?"

"Now be quiet and eat!" said Foula.

"Bones," answered Doup. "That's what's left."

But that night when he lay in his bed, it wasn't a skull with empty eye sockets he saw.

It was a head in flesh and blood with a pair of blue, blue eyes and a dark forelock, which fell down constantly, every time it was pushed back.

2

The horse skull sat at the end of the table and grinned at them with its old, yellow teeth. A hole had been drilled in its forehead, and there stood a straight, pale candle that waited to be lit as soon as darkness came.

It was the last day of the year. The table had been scoured white and set for everyone who lived in Crow Cove. Doup was chopping cabbage when Rossan came in.

He had brought a bowl of apples, which he placed on the table. Rossan was the oldest person in Crow Cove but had come to live there the most recently. He had a small orchard near his house up the stream. He sat down in a chair and polished every apple with his woolen shirtsleeve until they all lay shining red in the bowl. Afterward he pulled a comb out of his pocket and carefully combed his gray hair and his little, pointy beard. The door opened and a young man came in.

"So, Tink, what are you bringing?" asked Rossan, and stuck his comb in his pocket.

"Chewfish," Tink answered. He was the fisherman in Crow Cove.

He put down the dried lumpfish, pulled out a large knife, and began to cut the fish into paper-thin strips. Foula came over and set down a platter. She dried her hands on her apron and surveyed the table with satisfaction while she pushed a gray curl back into the knot on top of her head. A moment later it had fallen down again.

Frid and Cam came up from the stream with full water buckets, clean, red faces, and water-combed hair.

Finally Myna and her sweetheart, Kotka, arrived, sweaty and laughing, with a platter covered with a dish towel. Kotka pulled the cloth aside, revealing a steaming, cooked brined goose surrounded by thin curls of horseradish.

Foula hung the teakettle on the hook in the fireplace and went to get a jug of brandy from the bedroom. Then the table was ready.

"I'll light the candle in a moment," said Frid. "So if anyone has an errand outside, now is the time."

Foula sat down and put her arm around Cam.

"Do you have to pee?" she asked.

He shook his head.

"We can't let the Dark Night in once we've lit the candle," she explained. "So I've put a pot over in the corner."

"Stop it, Ma."

He wriggled away from her.

"Maybe it's the draft that we need to keep out most of all," said Frid. "The light must not go out."

Foula got up and blew out all the other candles, so only the glow from the hearth flickered in the room, and Frid lit the candle in the skull.

They all held their breath while the little flame hesitantly grew bigger. Its glow danced across the broad brow and left the eye sockets in the dark. Cam gasped.

"It's as if it's looking at us."

"Come on," said Foula. "Now we're going to celebrate!"

It was a long night. They ate and played games. Cam was the first to give up and fall asleep on the settle when the candle had burned a third of the way down.

Doup had decided to stay awake until Light Morning, but he was freezing and his eyes stung and it didn't help to rub them anymore.

"Come on!" invited Frid, and patted the settle next to him.

Doup lay down, but decided to keep his eyes open. If he closed them, then he wouldn't be able to open them again. He pulled his blanket up and lay gazing at his father.

Frid's light hair had turned mostly gray, but his eyes were still just as blue as Ravnar's. He leaned forward with his elbows on his knees and stared into the glowing fire on the hearth. His face took on a warm, red glow.

"What was I called before I was called Doup? What's my real name?"

"Alek," Frid answered without taking his eyes from the fire. "We named you Alek—your mother and I, a long time ago—before she died."

He leaned forward and took a piece of driftwood from the basket and placed it on the embers.

"I think it was Ravnar's idea," he said.

The flames caught and lit up the little flock sitting in a semicircle and warming themselves while they waited for the night to be over—for the old year to die—for a lighter time to come.

Over on the table, the candle had burned halfway down.

He was called Alek, the night was long, and his eyes slid shut.

He still had the name inside when he woke up. This foreign, sharp, angled name, totally different from Doup, which was childishly small and round—like a marble on the tongue.

It was Light Morning and outside the sun was shining. The parlor was empty, the candle had long since burned down, and the table had been cleared. He put on his boots to go home.

The wind was coming from the land, so the cove was sheltered by the hillcrest. The sun was high in the sky and had long been warming the stones and making the air mild. Not a person could be seen, but Glennie spotted him from the other side of the stream and ran to meet him, tail wagging.

He squatted and let the dog lick his ear, while he ran his fingers through the black, bristling coat and forward to her chest with its little white fan.

"Alek, can you say Alek?"

The dog answered with a jump and a deep yap, and he laughed.

"Yes, that's right," he said, and scratched her behind the ear.

When he got up, the dog ran ahead, once in a while stopping to turn and check that he was following. He stopped by the stream and hollowed his hands and lifted cold water up to his face. Glennie ran across the bridge and over to the front of the house where Alek lived with Myna and Kotka. She remained lying there when he stepped inside.

He carefully opened the door to the parlor. The sunshine made the yellow, varnished furniture shine like honey; the rifle hung in its place over the hearth, and Myna and Kotka lay sleeping in the wide bed in the corner.

They lay in each other's arms under the soft brown blanket made of skins. Kotka's hair stood out in all directions and looked completely white next to Myna's dark mane. He had bowed his head toward hers, his forehead resting on her temple, as if he was breathing her in while sleeping.

Alek stood looking at them for a little while. He knew exactly how she smelled—of thyme, seaweed, and wood smoke. He had slept there next to her both when he was little and also when he had grown bigger. She opened her eyes and looked at him; then she smiled and fell back to sleep again smiling.

He tiptoed out of the parlor and opened the door to his own room under the stairs. The bed was made up and covered by a woolen blanket. In front of it on the floor lay an old brown goatskin, its hairs worn away in the middle. His clothes hung on a rack on the wall, and on the window ledge stood a little spotted wooden cow with only one ear.

He shut the door and went to the room at the other side of the house. It was cool in there with a smoky smell from legs of lamb and bunches of dried flatfish hanging from the ceiling.

He found some cold potatoes that had been baked in the embers on the hearth. He split several open with his knife and forced the yellow masses out of the burned jackets and gnawed them clean.

The peels he brought along to the hens, who were scratching in the top of the manure pile. They pecked at the potato scraps and then followed him into the stable, which he mucked out, first the empty stall and then under the two big horses and the cow. He gave the animals water and forked fresh hay down from the loft for them.

A shadow fell across the door. Frid came in. He went over to the cow and began to scratch its forehead.

"It was sad about your little horse. Do you miss him?"

"I miss Ravnar more." Ravnar had gone to live in Last Harbor after Myna chose Kotka instead of him.

"Yes ... Ravnar," said Frid, and let his hand drop. "I wonder how he's doing."

The cow pushed him, and he lifted his hand and continued to rub its forehead.

"Maybe I should go up to visit him."

"I want to come," said Alek, and stood up straight.

"We could go with Eidi back to Last Harbor, when she comes to trade. There should be room for two more in that big boat."

The light was white when they stepped out of the dark stable with the hens underfoot. Frid went back to the house, and Alek drifted along the stream down to the beach where the wind reached him with the smell of fresh water and earth.

A gull walked along pecking at the seaweed, and Alek picked up a stone and hit it. Dazed, it flapped its wings upward, dropped a couple of feathers, and disappeared in the bright light.

3

The hail chased the hens back into the stable. Small marbles of ice hit the ground and shot up again as Alek moved along the dancing white carpet. He was on his way down to the beach because the boat from Last Harbor had appeared.

Six big men each sat at an oar and struggled to get the boat into the cove. Eidi could be seen at the stern with the first mate. It looked as if the boat was landing over and over in the same trough between the waves, but its growing size showed that it was getting closer. The sun broke through a sliver in the cloud cover, and the golden light chased the blue-black hailstorm out to sea, where the wind rippled the surface before it quickly disappeared.

Now Tink and Frid were also on their way to the beach. Foula appeared in the doorway with her shawl up around her ears. Cam ran after Frid while trying to button his coat as Foula was shouting for him to do. He gave up and stood still, stamping his feet impatiently while the buttons teased his small, fat fingers. Foula caught up with him and helped.

The boat scraped the beach. The two boatmen in front jumped out and grabbed hold of the railing. They pulled the boat forward toward land across planks placed to prevent the keel from digging too deeply into the layer of small dark pebbles.

In no time the boat stood high up on land. Eidi, who now managed the store in Last Harbor, jumped into her mother Foula's arms, and Cam clung to her legs. She bent down and kissed his round cheeks.

Then it was Tink's turn. Eidi pulled off his knit cap and ruffled his light brown hair and then she grabbed him by the shoulders and shook him.

"Oh, Tinkerlink, how you're growing," she said, laughing. He was half a head taller than her.

She said hello to the others, and finally she took hold of a strapping blond youth and pulled him over to Frid and Foula.

"This is Sigge," she said, and the giant took off his knit cap and stuck out his hand and smiled with his whole ruddy face.

The sliver of light in the sky had disappeared and the darkness had drawn nearer. Everyone helped empty the boat, big packages and sacks were dragged up to the house, and afterward Tink showed all the boatmen to his room at the potato house, where they could see to their own needs.

Alek carried a big package tied with a sturdy string. He stuck his nose into the smooth, speckled paper and took in the smell of smoked bacon.

Glennie came dancing toward him and wanted to smell, too. Myna and Kotka were on their way down from the hillcrest, where they had been up to check on the sheep. Myna had the shotgun and a couple of rabbits over her shoulder. Yet another wet nose fought its way to the delicious-smelling package. Rossan's dog, Glennierossa, had run on ahead, and a little later Rossan appeared.

The little house was noisily full of people when the door was finally shut on the next hail shower, which came drifting in with the darkness.

The boat lay heavily in the shallow water, loaded with bales of wool, deer- and goatskins, tanned sheepskins, sacks of rabbit furs, yarn, knitted socks and caps, and eiderdown, and baskets of root vegetables and wooden toy animals that Tink had carved, and a woven cage with a goose and a gander inside, who were setting out on their first journey away from the little cove.

Everything was ready for departure. Alek ran home to collect the skin satchel Myna had sewn for him. She had greased it with fat to keep the water out and had helped him pack it.

Now she came into the hallway holding a very small skin pouch, which she hung around his neck. He opened it and peeked inside and saw the glow from a couple of gold coins.

"So you can manage," said Myna, "if something should happen—or if someone needs your help. And take good care of yourself! Don't trust just anyone, and stick to people who make you feel comfortable!"

She looked penetratingly at him with her dark-blue eyes, which seemed almost black in the dim hallway. She smiled.

"I sound like an old woman," she said, and threw her arms around him and gave him a hug. "Good-bye, little one." Her voice was hoarser than usual.

"I won't be gone that long."

"You never know," she said, and let go.

Kotka came out of the parlor and took the leather satchel and slung it onto his shoulder, and together they all three went down to the waiting boat.

When they got there, Sigge took hold of him without a word and lifted him on board, as if he was another sack of socks. Kotka threw Alek's leather satchel after him and he caught it at the last moment.

Six hands waved from shore and three from the boat. The men grabbed the oars, and soon they were out of the cove. The sail was hoisted, the wind was at their backs, and Crow Cove disappeared from sight.

Alek was cold and wet when they drew close to Last Harbor. The wind, which pushed the boat along at a violent clip, had sent shower after shower in their wake. Ahead of them the waves boiled around some reefs at the end of a rocky spit that stuck out from land.

"Last Farewell," yelled Sigge.

"Furl the sail!" the first mate ordered, and now they had to use the oars to manage the point.

The men at the stern pulled steadily through the seething waves and turned the boat out toward the sea. A wave hit the side and water slammed over them. It poured off the men's beards.

"Row, you lazy dogs!" yelled the first mate.

All six struggled, gazes blank with effort. Then one of them began to chant in a deep voice in time with the long pulls:

> *"Row to the rolling sea*
> *Row with the fish below*
> *Row o'er herring and bream*
> *Row o'er cod and ling..."*

They rounded the reef, where the waves swirled, exposing the black rock at their base. Alek could feel a light scraping against the side of the boat and pulled away.

"Sit still!" snarled the man behind him.

> "...*row to the cabin*
> *Row to the old lady*
> *Row to the bed*
> *and...*"

"Shut your trap," yelled Sigge. "Save your vulgar ditties for poorer company than ours."

The man fell silent. Everyone grew silent. They had cleared the point and the boat raced along over the calm, protected water beyond it. Two burning tar torches marked the entrance to the harbor, and behind them were golden squares lit in the dusk; a final rain shower hit them from the side and pulled the night along with it. The lights swiftly came closer. On land awaited warmth and shelter and full pots.

4

Alek's legs were stiff; the world rocked beneath him when he finally stood on the pier. The men at once began to empty the boat in the light from a couple of torches.

Eidi came over to him and Frid, but she didn't take her eyes off the work.

"Don't you want to come home with me? Of course, it'll take a little while ... Watch those geese; those are live animals! But I have ..."

"You're busy," said Frid. "We'll try to find Ravnar."

"You can't. They're at sea."

"Then we'll try the inn. Let's go!"

Alek staggered along. Frid put out his arm so Alek could lean on him, but he wanted to manage himself.

There were no other guests in the parlor of the inn. A woman came over to greet them.

"It's a quiet night when the boats are at sea. I don't have all that much to offer, but you won't go hungry. First you'll get a warm cup of tea and then I'll see what I can rustle up."

She brought them both mugs of tea and disappeared into the kitchen. A big log crackled peacefully in the fireplace, and a clock on the mantel chimed three slight, crisp strikes. On either side of the clock lay two big pink conch shells, and on the walls hung pictures: colored drawings of strange fruits and, on the wall right next to Alek, a girl with black curly hair, herding a flock of goats on a mountainside above a turquoise-blue sea.

The woman returned with a big bowl of fish soup for each of them. They ate in silence, the wind howling around the house and the clock chiming at regular intervals. The woman came back and removed the empty bowls and gave them each a plate with lamb chops and a smooth mash of white beans.

Finally they were served a kind of tart filled with prunes and more cups of strong tea. The woman put three glasses on the table and asked if they would like some warm, spiced wine. Frid said yes, thank you, for them both. The woman got the pitcher and poured.

She took a glass herself and sat down in a big chair in front of the hearth. She placed her feet with their swollen ankles on a stool and sighed. Holding his glass, Frid nodded to Alek.

"Now you must be both full and warm," he said.

"Very full and very tired," Alek admitted, and leaned back in his chair and sipped the hot, sweet brew.

Frid turned to the woman.

"That was a delicious meal," he said, and the woman nodded slightly in thanks. "Tell me, do you know a younger fisherman named Ravnar?"

"Ravnar Heavy Heart we call him," she answered. "Yes, I know him. He has rented a little cabin from me down on the beach."

At that moment there was a faint knock on the window, no louder than the sound of a fingernail or the beak of a sparrow. The woman started, jolting her glass, so a few red drops landed on her white apron.

"What was that?" asked Alek.

"People say," answered Frid, "that if there is a knock on the window three times in a night then a ship has gone down."

"The last time I heard that sound someone had gotten lost in the fog. But let's not talk about that."

She got up and went into the kitchen and came back without her apron.

"Do you have a place where we can sleep?" asked Frid.

"Yes, you can have the best in the house; you're the only guests."

She threw open the door to a room next to the parlor. There were two big beds with white sheets and a little table between them, two armchairs in front of a fireplace, and on a small sideboard with a marble top stood a dish of soap, a wash basin, and a water pitcher.

"Should I light the fire?"

Frid shook his head. So she lit the candles in the candlesticks, wished them a good night, and left.

"Isn't this expensive?" Alek wanted to know.

"Yes," said Frid as he pulled off his pants. "But then you'll have tried it."

Alek was already lying under the cool eiderdown comforter. The bed lifted him gently up and down like a rolling sea, and behind his eyelids were pictures of South Sea fruits and herding girls and boatmen. Frid blew out the candles and climbed into the other bed.

Right before Alek fell asleep, he thought he heard a faint tapping on the window, but perhaps it was just a dream that began as the bed rocked him off onto the night's sail.

The town was checked in black and white: whitewashed houses and black tarred sheds crept up along narrow streets and alleys. The boats had come in, and long rows of women stood cleaning fish on old doors and broad planks resting on sawhorses.

The gulls dipped and screamed around them, and children put the cleaned cod in big salt troughs and the liver in barrels, where it would end up as cod-liver oil. The whole harbor smelled of fish.

Frid asked around—all the boats had come in. The innkeeper had told them how to get to Ravnar's cabin, and they continued along the harbor up over a cliff and down to the beach on the other side.

Here you couldn't see any houses other than the cabin that lay in the inner hollow of the point that stuck out into the sea, the point Sigge had called Last Farewell. A little stream had hollowed out a course behind the cliff and across the beach not far from there. Between the stream and the cabin lay a pile of driftwood.

The cabin was built of black tarred wood. A whitewashed brick gable with a chimney faced the sea. No smoke rose from the chimney, the roof was covered by worn peat, the small windows were grubby with sea fog, and the cabin seemed abandoned.

But inside in the sleeping alcove they found Ravnar, asleep and ash-gray with exhaustion in the cold room. On the table lay a heel of bread—which must have lain there for many days, it was hard as rock—and a few slices of sausage, which had curled up at both ends. The milk in the glass was so thick that it had separated.

On the floor lay his clothes, greasy and heavy with seawater, making muddy puddles. Frid found an old canvas sack in a corner and gathered the clothes in it. Then he went through the cabin and took all the laundry he could find.

"The sheets will have to wait until he wakes up."

He gave Alek the sack and asked him to take it up to the innkeeper to see if she knew a washerwoman. He would stay behind and light a fire and clean.

"And then stop by Eidi's and buy tea and sugar and candles, and a bucket of soap and a scrubbing brush, bread, butter, and cheese and whatever else you can think of."

He handed Alek a gold coin. Then he lifted a pipe from the table.

"And a little pouch of tobacco—and a jug of beer. Can you carry all that?"

"Easily," answered Alek, and he hoisted the sack on his back and hurried to town.

5

All life took place in the harbor; up here among the houses and cabins you didn't see anyone except an occasional housewife behind a polished window or a glimpse of a rat rounding a corner.

The innkeeper had sent Alek to the middle of town, where she knew a washerwoman. He found her by sniffing his way, because a strong smell of steam and soap came out of the building and down the lane, and the courtyard was covered with clotheslines and sweet-smelling sheets, flapping in the wind.

He handed over the heavy sack and followed the

road along the stream down toward the harbor again. Small steps, carved into the cliff, led to the water, and on the other side lay a long row of houses. Several of them were built together, gable to gable, so only the chimneys revealed where one ended and the next began. A flock of jackdaws chattered above his head and a cat streaked across the road with a small, silvery fish in its mouth.

A bridge crossed the water, and he walked to the middle of it and looked up at the stream, until the sun made him close his eyes and throw his head back and enjoy the warmth on his skin. Somewhere a baby began to cry, then fell silent a moment later.

He finally found Eidi's house by the road that led to the harbor square. It was a long building with living quarters at one end and the store at the other. It was taller than the other houses because it had a basement with windows at street level. Behind it lay stables, sheds, and storage rooms. A staircase led up to the store.

Eidi was alone when he stepped in. She stood at a desk writing numbers in a fat black book. Her hair was put up in a bun at the nape of her neck, and her

dress was light brown with a pattern of little rose-
buds and leaves and a cream-colored lace collar.

A small gold pin held the collar together, and on
her little finger was a gold ring with a green stone.
She looked so grownup and elegant. When she saw
him, she smiled and came over.

"I need to buy some things," he said, searching
his pocket for the gold coin and placing it on the
counter.

"That's a big coin, but you don't have to pay for
this," she said, and offered him a hard candy from
a tin.

He took it in his mouth and gave up on talking for
a while because it was so big that there was no room
to move his tongue. He looked around.

He had never seen so many different things gathered in one place. Dress fabric, knitting supplies, rope
and fishing lines, knives, hooks, pots, pans, barrels of
herring and salt pork, sacks of flour and sugar, oats
and potatoes and . . .

"Did you find Ravnar?"

He nodded.

"It's a hard life." Eidi's brow furrowed in a small

horizontal line. "Wouldn't you rather stay here with me?"

He shook his head. The furrow grew deeper.

"What was it you needed?"

Alek ground the candy between his teeth to free up his mouth. At that moment the door opened and Sigge stepped in. Eidi's face lit up in a smile. He came over to the counter and placed a wooden case before her.

"Can you use this?"

The chest was made of light, reddish yellow wood with a large E worked into the lid in an almost black wood and with a rhombus in whitish yellow mother-of-pearl on either side of the letter. She turned the key in the lock and opened it. The inside was divided into a row of small and a row of large compartments.

"For money, I was thinking," said Sigge.

"You're right about that," said Eidi, and let her hand glide across the lid.

"Then it's yours."

Sigge lifted his knitted cap and disappeared out the door.

"Where were we?" asked Eidi, but the smile remained in her eyes. Alek began.

She found the items for him and suggested he also buy six freshly laid eggs that she had received that same morning and a piece of freshly smoked bacon.

"He needs something warm. You have to come here to eat one night—next time he's in port."

"But he's in port now."

"They are going out again the day after tomorrow."

She carefully packed his purchases in a canvas sack and gave him the eggs in a little basket.

"Do you have anything to sleep on?" Without waiting for an answer she got out two blankets, which she rolled together like a sausage and gave him tied together with rope to go across his shoulder.

"You can return them when you leave."

He staggered toward the door.

"You need your change," she yelled after him.

"Can't I leave it here with you?"

"Of course," she said, laughing, and ran after him and stood on the staircase.

"Do you need help?"

"No," he called without stopping or turning

around, though he was sure that she was still there waving to him.

"Goodbye," he yelled before he turned the corner, but by then she must have shut the door.

Late in the afternoon, the heat and the smell of bacon and soap finally got Ravnar to open his eyes. He stuck out his head and looked around in confusion before he caught sight of Frid and Alek.

"I didn't expect a visit," he said, and pulled his head in again.

After a while, he said from behind the curtain, "Why are you here?"

Alek didn't know how to answer and Frid apparently didn't either. Then Ravnar appeared again and looked around one more time.

"What have you done?" he asked.

"Cleaned," said Alek. "And shopped and gotten your clothes washed. They're hanging there."

He pointed at the line that was strung from wall to wall in front of the hearth.

"How are you going to get them dry by tomorrow morning?"

"They are almost dry. They've been hanging there for hours."

"Hmmm," Ravnar noted doubtfully. "And what about now?"

"Put on a blanket," Frid suggested, and threw one of Eidi's thick blankets over to him.

He caught it and threw it back and turned around and dug his own worn one from the alcove. Then he sat down in the chair by the table.

Frid handed him a plate with fried bacon, two eggs sunny-side up, and a big slice of bread, and Ravnar wolfed it down. It was all gone in an instant.

Then Frid served Alek and himself, while Ravnar continued to eat whatever was on the table. He washed down the food with one mug of tea after another. He didn't stop eating until there was nothing left.

"That's the best meal I've had in a long time," he said, and offered Alek and Frid something that might have been a tiny smile.

"Do you mind if we stay here for a few days?" asked Frid.

"If you want to see me, you might have to stay more than a few days."

He ran his hand through his longish black hair.

"Then that's what we'll do," said Frid, and pushed the pipe and a little pouch of tobacco over to him.

And while Ravnar sat in front of the hearth with his legs up on a stool and let the bluish smoke rise in long spirals, Frid and Alek constructed a broad, low bed in the corner by the hearth. They collected bone-dry seaweed high up on the beach and placed it under one of the blankets as a mattress; they'd cover themselves with the other one.

Frid sent Alek up to the innkeeper for a pail of warm soup. Ravnar ate a single bowlful and drank a mug of beer. Then he disappeared behind the curtain and a little later they heard him breathing deeply.

Frid sat staring into the fire. Alek glanced at him. He looked so serious. He turned his head and looked at Alek.

"Well, should we see about getting some sleep?"

* * *

Alek couldn't remember ever having slept with Frid. He smelled different, a bit harsh like tarry soot, and he was big and heavy so that the boards bent when he turned over.

Alek lay awake for a long time and stared into the darkness, listening to the two sleeping men, before finally drifting off.

6

The rocks were white with cod and the intense and sour smell blew across the town. Alek was on his way home with the heavy sack of sheets that he had picked up from the washerwoman. He crossed the little bridge and continued down past the inn. The innkeeper appeared in the door as he went by.

"You, little man," she called, and he set down the sack and walked over to her.

"Alek," he said.

"I need help in the kitchen. I'll pay you with all

you can eat for dinner—also for Ravnar and your father."

"I just have to take the washing home first."

The woman nodded, and Alek took the sack and hurried out to the cabin. Frid didn't object and soon Alek was standing in the inn's kitchen.

The side of beef was so large that he could barely turn it in the tub. He rubbed it with a mixture of salt and sugar and spices that he had ground to a fine powder in the big mortar. The meat smelled sweetly of blood and spicy from pepper and juniper berries. The door of the cool larder was open to the kitchen, where the innkeeper stood chopping onions.

"Tomorrow there'll be moisture around it and then it has to be rubbed with the juice every day for ten days." The woman rinsed her hands in the water basin and dried them and her eyes on her apron. She filled two pails from pots on the stove, put lids on them, and placed a piece of bread next to them. Then she sat down on a stool with her hands in her lap.

"That's enough for today. There's mutton stew in one and fish soup in the other."

Alek stuck the bread under his arm, grabbed the pails by the handles, and walked out into the darkness. The faint glow from the inn's window led him to the path over the cliff, but then everything grew black. He felt his way forward with the tip of his boot, but the gravel slipped under his feet.

The wind pushed him and let him go, then gave him a new push. One of his feet stepped into nothing, while he held himself upright on the other, swaying. His hands clutched the pail handles, and he spread his arms out, letting the bread crash down from the cliff, and managed to step back to safe ground and fumble on.

From the top of the cliff he could make out two yellowish squares farther down the beach. He knew that the cabin's door was right between them and steered in that direction.

Ravnar sat with a blanket around him in the chair in front of the hearth; Frid sat on the bed mending one of Ravnar's shirts.

"You were lucky to get work," said Ravnar without turning his head. "She's a good cook."

"I think it was just for today."

Alek placed the pails on the table and got out bowls and spoons.

"She hasn't had any help in the kitchen since old Enver fell to his death. She'll probably need you again."

Ravnar turned his chair toward the table and lifted the lid of the soup pail. Frid pulled the end of the thread to the back of the shirt and came over and sat down.

They started with the pail of soup; they continued with the potatoes and mutton until nothing was left. Alek set the bowls outside the door so they could wash them in the stream the next day. Frid put more logs on the fire.

The wind grew stronger and shook the house, and only the heat of the fire prevented it from forcing its way down the chimney; the raindrops pounded on the windows, then the rain turned to hail that smashed against the glass.

"We probably won't make it out tomorrow," said Ravnar, and began to fill his pipe.

Alek found a burning twig in the fire and handed it to him.

"When the weather allows, we have to go back," said Frid. "Do you want to come?"

Ravnar shook his head and sucked in the blue smoke before letting it drift slowly toward the ceiling.

"I have nothing more to do in Crow Cove."

He had not been there since Myna chose Kotka instead of him.

Alek moved a bit closer to the fire. The flames licked up around the wood and sent a wavy light out into the room. The light rose and fell. It hit Frid on one side of his face and left the other in darkness.

"Since your mother died," he began, "I may have been happy, but there has always been something in me that at the same time has been infinitely sorrowful."

Alek sat completely still, Ravnar smoked, Frid cleared his throat.

"That's how it will always be, I know that now."

"That's different; she died," objected Ravnar.

"Is it?" asked Frid.

Ravnar bent forward and scraped out his pipe over the hearth. Then he knocked it hard against his palm so that the last bits of tobacco fell out. He turned his head and looked up at Alek with a gleam in his eye.

"And what about you, Doup? Do you have a sweetheart?"

"Alek. My name is Alek now." He clenched his fists on the tabletop. "I was called Doup when I was little."

"And now you're big, and you haven't found a sweetheart yet."

Alek threw himself on Ravnar and managed to give him a couple of punches in the shoulder before Ravnar grabbed his wrists and held him in a viselike grip. Alek fought to get loose.

"Are you kicking?"

Ravnar got up, so the blanket slid down, and he lifted Alek up and hugged him to his naked body. Alek wriggled like a fish and hammered away on Ravnar's back, but Ravnar threw him onto his shoulder and carried him over to the bed and placed his entire heavy weight on top of him.

"I give in," panted Alek, and Ravnar stood up.

"You've gotten stronger since I saw you last," he

said, and stuck out his hand and pulled Alek to his feet.

Then he picked up his blanket and wrapped himself in it.

"Well," he said. "Are you offering a mug of beer?"

When they woke up the next morning a yellow-gray light forced its way through the small panes. The sea was whipped to a froth that clung to the glass and flew in white clumps across the black stones of the beach.

There was a knock at the door; outside stood a little boy, asking if Alek would come up to the inn again today. All the ships were in harbor, and the inn was full.

Alek grabbed the empty pails and followed him. Up on the cliff the wind was so fierce that the boy reached for Alek's hand in order not to be blown over.

"How did you manage the trip out here?" asked Alek.

"I crawled," yelled the boy.

The inn's parlor was thick with voices and smoke when Alek made his way through to the kitchen.

Sweaty and red-faced, the innkeeper was sitting down, frying lamb chops in a pan on the hearth.

"Chop me off another ten!" She nodded her head in the direction of the larder. "And then you can start rubbing the meat!"

A rack of lamb was lying on the wooden block with a big meat ax next to it. Alek squared his shoulders and lifted the ax over his head and let it fall. He produced a very fat lamb chop. He fetched the big knife and split it in half. The next one turned out better, and the final one was exactly as it was supposed to be.

He worked without a break the whole day, and when it began to get dark, he asked the woman for permission to leave.

"Yes, that road isn't good in the dark," she answered. "But then you'll have to come a bit earlier tomorrow."

He promised. She ladled white bean mash into one pail and placed six lamb chops on top. In the other, there was potato soup with bread on the side.

He tied his scarf around his waist and stuck the bread underneath it and lifted the pails.

Far out to the west the cloud cover had let go of the sea, and a shining section of reddish yellow sky appeared. The storm had subsided and left behind a noisy swell. A star blinked from the sky island in the sea of clouds, and the cabin's eyes greeted him.

7

Come back with us!" pleaded Alek yet another time.

The day's first gray light seeped in through the half-open door along with the smell of saltwater and seaweed.

"You could also stay here," said Ravnar casually, and took his knife from the table and put it in its sheath. "Otherwise, goodbye."

He quietly closed the door behind him. Alek tore it open.

"Goodbye," he yelled after the dark figure, which lifted its hand without turning around.

The boards shifted in the bed, and Frid came over and stood in the doorway next to him. Ravnar was already on his way down behind the cliff.

"I don't like leaving him," said Frid. "But what can I do?"

"I could stay here."

Frid shook his head.

"I could come back with Eidi in the fall."

Frid looked at him.

"I could work at the inn. Then he would get some proper food."

"I don't want you to fish."

Frid shut the door.

"I won't," promised Alek.

Frid walked over and squatted in front of the hearth. He poked at the embers and put more logs on.

"I'll talk to the innkeeper and Eidi about it," he said.

The flock of jackdaws was in the air and holding a conference on the rooftops. There was smoke in the chimneys and there were little urchins in the yards when Alek accompanied Frid to the edge of town.

He would take the inland road and in a few days he would be back in Crow Cove.

"Take care of yourself!" Frid put a hand on Alek's shoulder. "And take care of Ravnar!"

Then he pulled Alek to his itchy wool jacket for a short moment and let him go again.

Alek stood looking after him, and every time Frid turned around, they waved at each other. Alek sat down on a rock at the edge of the road, and there he remained until he could no longer see his father. Now he was alone.

During the day he was busy at the inn, but all too often when he came home in the evening the cabin stood empty and dark on the beach. Still he didn't want to accept the innkeeper's offer to sleep over on the bench in the kitchen.

Every evening he carried food home and started a fire and prepared for the next time that Ravnar would come home. He usually stayed home one night, at the most two, before he set off again.

* * *

"Tap, tap," was the sound against the pane.

Alek sat up in bed with a start and listened out into the darkness. The wind whipped around the chimney and along the roof on a hunt for cracks. The smell from the sleeping fire hung in the air, and from somewhere the cold came creeping. He pulled his blanket closer and lay down again.

The pictures came and went: the big piece of beef in the wooden trough with the bloody juice at the bottom, Frid's back on its way through the gray landscape, the jackdaws who sought each other out above the town, the gulls that fought at sea, Ravnar's black hair against his folded arm when he sat sleeping at the table, wave after wave after wave all the way to the end of the world . . .

"Tap, tap."

A ship goes down, a man gets lost in the fog, the stones roll out over the edge of the cliff. Wide awake now, Alek tumbled from sleep's fragile shelf down into the pitch dark.

He lay stock-still so as not to reveal to the dark that he was there. But the darkness stared straight at his face and placed its heavy hand on his thigh. It breathed the smell of ash and dried seaweed into his nostrils. It breathed deeply, so that the cabin's boards creaked.

"Tap, tap."

And the ship went down.

When he left the cabin, he stepped into an even greater darkness. Everything was black: sky, sea, and the rocks under his feet. But in the black there was one little point of light, and when he came closer, he saw there were two fires that burned all the way out at the end of the point, all the way out at Last Farewell's fingertips.

Alek bent forward against the wind and began to fight his way out there. Slowly his eyes grew accustomed to the dark, and he began to glimpse a line of planks and barrels, sacks and chests, that were being ground against the beach by the waves.

Then he caught sight of the wreck. It had lodged onto a reef and had broken in half. The waves threw themselves at it, pulling and tearing and tugging.

But the hull would not be budged, only the loose

parts drifted toward land, and now Alek could see that one of them was a drowned sailor who lay face-down, staring into the deep. A moment later he disappeared.

Then Alek realized that the bonfires had been lit as if to show the entrance to a harbor. But here you did not sail into light and food and warmth; here you sailed to your death.

Once in a while it looked as if the wind would blow out the fires, but each time they took hold again. In the wandering light on the beach three men walked around wresting boxes and barrels from the waves.

Alek carefully slipped behind a big rock, where he could hide and keep an eye on what was happening.

A man came out of the sea, crawling on all fours up toward land. But the wave would not let go of him; it grabbed hold of his legs and pulled him down onto his stomach, yet he managed to get up again and continue crawling.

The largest of the three men on the beach walked over to him. But instead of offering him a hand, the man grabbed an oar and hit the shipwrecked man with all his might on the back of his bowed head. The man sank down, and at the same moment there was a scream by Alek's ear.

He turned his head and glimpsed a pair of dark eyes in a pale, wet face. It had to be someone from the ship.

The figure attempted to get up, but Alek grabbed hold of it and pulled it with him behind the rock and placed a hand over the unknown mouth.

If the three men on the beach had heard the scream, they would both be finished. Nausea poured over him, and his heart beat so that his chest hurt.

For a long time Alek lay motionless waiting for the blow that would send him into the great darkness forever. But nothing happened. He moved his hand and the shipwrecked figure was silent.

Then he carefully stuck his head out and looked up over the rock. The shipwrecked man was gone; the wave had gotten its prey.

The three men were still busy salvaging wreckage from the water's edge with long boat hooks. Slowly they worked their way closer and closer.

Alek pointed in the direction of the cabin and

started to carefully crawl away, and the shipwrecked person crawled along behind him. After a while he looked back and could no longer see either the men or the bonfires. They must have extinguished them. Then he got up, pulling the stranger with him, and hand in hand they ran over to the cabin.

He slammed the door behind them and fumbled his way to the candlestick on the table and lit the candle.

And there she stood: the goatherd above the turquoise sea, with black curls from which the water was pouring, wearing a dress that had been torn. Blood trickled from the many scrapes on her arms and legs and face, creating a marbled pattern on her white skin.

He found a towel for her and a blanket she could wrap around herself, and then he turned his back so she could change in privacy.

With a little tap on the shoulder she told him that she was done. She had spread the wet clothes across a chair. He pointed to the alcove opening, and she sat down on the bed with her legs dangling over the side.

He was just about to sit down beside her when

someone knocked on the door. He quickly pushed her into the alcove and pulled the curtain before he threw a blanket around himself and opened the door.

Sigge stood outside.

"I came by and saw that the light was on here in the middle of the night. Is everything okay?"

"I just had a nightmare."

"Oh," said Sigge. "What did you dream?"

"About a sound."

Sigge glanced past him into the parlor.

"It can be scary to be alone. Do you want me to come in?"

Alek shook his head.

"I was just about to go to bed. Thanks anyway."

"Well, good night then."

Alek closed the door and hurried over to blow out the candle.

8

Alek's shirt was too small and Ravnar's old pants way too big for the young woman. Alek found her a belt she could keep them up with. Then he continued making breakfast.

"Would you like a fried egg?"

She looked at him completely lost. She must be able to say something. He pointed at himself.

"Alek."

He pointed at her.

"Thala," she answered.

Her voice was deep and soft. She dipped her finger

in the pitcher of milk and wrote her name on the table. After that they ate in silence. When they were done, she picked up her torn dress and made some motions with her hand as if she was sewing it.

He nodded and found a rusty sewing needle and a spool of thread in a small bowl above the hearth. He couldn't find scissors, so he gave her his knife.

Then he showed how he was going to lock the door from the outside so no one could come in while he was gone.

The remains of the wreck still stood on the reef, and there were many people on the beach collecting driftwood. All the boxes and barrels were gone. The thick cloud covering had opened up and let columns of light hit the surface of the sea. The waves had subsided, and only the swells hinted at their wildness in the night.

Alek hurried up over the cliff and down to the harbor. Many of the boats had arrived in the early daylight, and the women were already at work with their long, narrow knives. The air was spotted with gulls. But the boat that Ravnar had sailed with was missing.

He walked over to a boat where they were shoveling fish up onto the bed of a pushcart and asked after him.

"He got a hook caught in his hand," they told him. "They went to Eastern Harbor to have it cut out."

Alek thanked them for the message and walked to the inn. A big bucket of potatoes stood ready for him; they had to be peeled and sliced for the mutton stew. The innkeeper was sitting and cutting meat into cubes.

"The poor sailors," she said. "No one thinks of them; everyone just thinks of wreckage and lumber." She took a handful of meat and put it in the big iron pot. "And many go down, way too many."

"There was a bonfire on the beach last night."

She looked up at him, frightened.

"Don't speak out loud about that," she said. "I think that was what cost old Enver his life."

"Didn't he fall?"

"It was foggy. They say he took a wrong step, but he built the cabin on the beach over twenty-five years ago, and he made the trip home in pitch darkness night after night. What does fog mean then?"

She got up and washed her hands and came over to watch him work.

"Try to take off less potato with the peel! I know it's hard when they are so soft and mushy, but before long there'll be a shortage."

He tried. It took longer, but she had never rushed him. He looked up at her. She had sat down with a mug of tea and put her feet up on a stool.

"Help yourself to a mug if you like," she said.

He shook his head and continued peeling; she sipped the scalding tea. Her cheeks were red from the cold winters and the warmth of the fire.

"What's your name?" Alek asked suddenly.

She looked at him, surprised.

"You're the first person to ask me that since I arrived in Last Harbor. Everyone just calls me innkeeper, and my husband called me Ma. My name is Jona."

He wiped the starch from his fingers and poured a mug of tea for himself. She emptied hers and got up.

"And who will listen to someone whose name

they don't even want to know, so don't repeat my words! And don't tell anyone that you saw anything!"

There was a knock on the door. A couple of little girls stood outside with a big basket filled with strange orange balls.

"Mother told us to bring these to you, because she doesn't know what to use them for."

Jona picked one up.

"These must be oranges," she said. "I'd like to have them."

"There are a lot more down on the beach."

"Then go get another basketful."

Jona poured the fruit into a wooden trough and gave each of the girls a coin. Then she placed one of the oranges on the cutting board and sliced it like an onion. The thin, yellow juice spread across the white-scoured wood. She handed Alek one of the slices and took one herself.

The hard peel was bitter, the fruit tasted both sour and sweet at the same time. Alek had never tasted anything like it.

"What if we slice them and cook them with sugar?" he suggested.

Jona nodded.

"Let's try. Maybe they can be used as filling for tarts."

In the end, they decided that the orange, syrupy jam tasted best on bread.

Jona sent Alek to see if Eidi would like some for the store. Eidi agreed to try a few jars to see if people liked it.

"I need to buy something, too," said Alek. "Fabric for a dress for Myna."

"But she got fabric from me when I was there."

"It's supposed to be a present—from me."

"Oh, I see," said Eidi, and began to pull down the heavy rolls from the shelves. Black and dark-blue cloth, just one color or with a small pattern.

Alek caught sight of a roll with shiny, blue-green material, turquoise blue, with light-yellow fingers of seaweed that spread across it like filigree.

"That's it," he said, and pointed at the roll.

"I don't think she's going to like that."

"Please," said Alek.

"Well, it's your money," said Eidi, and measured the fabric.

"And thread and needle and scissors."

"But she has scissors," objected Eidi.

"She asked for a pair," said Alek, and got it all.

He also bought a little brown notebook with blank, yellowish paper and a pencil.

The rest of the day Alek and Jona cooked oranges. The little girls dragged up one basket after another.

When it began to get dark, Jona cut a thick slice of the cold roasted spiced beef and gave him a pail with potatoes and onions that had been baked in the ashes in the hearth. They had not had time to prepare anything else.

"Take a couple of oranges, too, if you'd like!" she said, and stuck one into each of his pockets.

He did not go home across the cliff but circled it, following the stream that led out to the beach. It was dark in the cabin when he went in, and when he lit the candle he could not see her.

"Thala," he called, and she stuck her head out from the alcove.

She came over to him and took his hand in greeting. She walked over to the door, knocked hard on it, and pulled at the handle, then ran back to the alcove and peeked out from behind the curtain. Then she pointed at one of the small, dirty windows, stepped out onto the floor, and made herself big and broad shouldered.

A man had been there, knocking. He had tried to open the door, but it was locked. Then he had looked in the window and had gone away again. It was good that she had hidden. And it was probably best not to clean the windows.

He handed her the package from Eidi's store and pointed at her. She unwrapped it and smiled when she saw the things he had bought. She held up the fabric and hugged it to her body like an embrace. He took the pencil and wrote her name on the little book. She grabbed his hand across the table and squeezed it.

But when he pulled the two oranges out of his pockets and handed them to her, she burst into tears.

9

On the first page of the little brown notebook Thala drew a town that rose from the sea up the side of a mountain. The houses had flat roofs and the town was speckled with trees and vines. The ships in the harbor had sails and were heavily loaded with freight. A bright sun sizzled in a cloudless sky.

On the next page she drew a single ship. She was very careful with the details, and Alek recognized the wreck. Underneath the ship she drew the cargo: oranges, some plants in bunches that Alek didn't know, perhaps herbs, large casks of wine, and jars and decorated ceramic bowls.

There wasn't enough room for everything, so she continued along the sides of the ship and on top, so that the drawing eventually resembled a square frame with an oval picture in the middle.

On the third page a man and a woman appeared with a little girl between them. Underneath the girl she wrote Thala. The woman, who must be her mother, had a long thick braid hanging down over one breast; her father had black hair and a beard and was tall and broad shouldered. He had rings in both ears.

The last drawing showed the same man crawling up onto a beach. In front of him a dark figure had raised an oar. A tear landed on his head. Thala got up and dried her eyes and began to pace back and forth across the floor like a caged animal.

Her reddish brown dress was veined by long rents, which she had mended with thousands of little stitches. She had tied her hair with a leather cord that she had found in the little bowl on the mantel.

Alek found the shirt and pants and handed them

to her along with a knit cap and pointed at the door. Seen from a distance she would look like a boy.

The beach had been plundered and abandoned; even the wreck was gone. The moon's silver light made even the smallest stone stand out clearly. Thala leaned her head back and looked at the starry sky. Together they walked along the water while the waves licked the stones.

A bird's cry cut through the clear air, and Thala pointed up at the seven sisters in the sky. Slowly she and Alek walked to the tip of the point.

Something blinked at the water's edge. Alek bent down to pick up a blue and white jar. The water ran from it through a hole in the bottom. When it was empty he handed it to Thala.

They walked home along the other side of the point and ended at the stream, where they got down on their knees and drank from hollowed hands.

Thala washed her face, then she walked a little way along the water and collected some mud. She closed the hole in the bottom of the jar with a small, uneven stone, before filling it with mud.

At home in the cabin she took one of the oranges and carefully peeled off the thick skin and divided the fruit into segments. Alek followed her lead. The bitterness was in the skin; peeled, it just tasted sweet and sour. Thala took three of the pips and pressed them into the wet dirt in the jar and placed it on a saucer on the window ledge.

The bodies of the shipwrecked drifted to shore one after another. A man with gold rings in both ears and black hair and a beard streaked with gray must have hit the rocks with great force because the back of his head was crushed.

There was also a woman among the dead. Her clothes had been ripped off so she was naked as a newborn when they found her, but a strong leather cord had managed to contain her long thick braid. Her fingers were swollen and her ring finger was missing.

The strangers were buried in the cemetery at the edge of town close to the inland road that led south. Nine stone piles covered the bodies of eight men and one woman, and only the birds sang at the burial.

It was Jona who knew.

Ravnar's ship returned, without Ravnar. He and the skipper had gotten into an argument, which had ended with Ravnar preferring to walk the whole long way from Eastern Harbor to Last Harbor rather than setting foot on the rotten old tub. One of the other crew members sought Alek out to tell him.

And Alek went out to the beach and threw stones at the cliffs and the waves and the gulls, at everything that lay still and everything that moved.

A couple of days later Jona came into the kitchen with a big, square piece of driftwood, beautifully rounded at the corners.

"Can you draw?" she asked.

"A bit."

"I was thinking of hanging a sign above the door— with a picture of a plate of lamb chops, a glass of wine, and some oranges on a white tablecloth or something like that. Can you manage that?"

Alek promised to buy paint and brushes at Eidi's and bring the sign home to see what he could do.

It was heavy and difficult to carry the paint and the wood and the food pail all down over the cliff, but the route around the stream was even longer. He staggered along, walking as carefully as he could.

A stone fell into the deep a bit behind him, down into the crack with water at the bottom where he had once dropped the bread. The stone hit the water with a hollow plop. Alek hurried on. The sun had set, and dusk had arrived. The light misty rain had brought the night closer and made the stones slippery.

He listened with his entire back, but didn't have time to hear anything before he was seized from behind by a pair of strong arms that held him upright so that he could neither move nor turn around. He leaned forward and plunged his teeth into the sleeve of a wool sweater and bit as hard as he could.

"You rotten kid," said Ravnar, laughing, and let him go.

*   *   *

When they stepped into the cabin, Ravnar halted at
the door with a start. Suddenly Alek realized how
odd it was for Thala to be standing there.

She looked so exotic with the deep, square neck
of her dress, which was cut close to her breasts and
then loosened and fell in deep folds toward the floor.
Her hair was gathered high on her head and a bunch
of small black curls had gotten loose and twisted
down along her white neck. She had a big piece of
driftwood in both hands and Alek understood that
she had heard their voices and gotten frightened. He
walked over to her and took the wood from her.
Then he grabbed her hand and pulled her over to
Ravnar. He pointed at him and said his name. She
nodded and put out her hand. Ravnar took it carefully in his with the slightly grubby bandage.

"And this is Thala," said Alek, while Ravnar blushed.

While they ate, Alek reported everything that he
knew. Ravnar listened and became more and more
angry.

"They're murderers," he exclaimed, and began to

walk up and down the floor. "And you haven't said anything to anyone?"

"No."

"That's probably best. We have to keep an eye on the beach so they can be caught in the act." He sat down again and breathed deeply. "That's the only thing we can do."

Thala walked over to him with a basin of warm water. She pointed at his hand; then she sat down and carefully undid the bandage. A deep flame-red wound went through his entire palm.

"You don't need to do that," objected Ravnar, and pulled his hand away, but she took hold of it again and placed it in the water, where she cleaned it.

Afterward she dried it and tied a clean white strip of cloth around it. She got up and emptied the basin outside the door.

"She can't stay here," declared Ravnar.

"Why not?"

"I don't want a woman in my house."

"She doesn't have anywhere else to live," said Alek.

Thala sat down on the edge of the alcove.

"Good night," she said gently in her odd accent, before she disappeared behind the curtain.

"And damn if she hasn't taken my bed, too—the witch!"

Alek couldn't help laughing, but stopped when he caught the dark look that Ravnar sent him.

10

Every night when Thala thought that Ravnar and Alek were sleeping she got up and stepped into Ravnar's old pants and Alek's too-small shirt, pulled the knit cap down around her ears, and walked out to the end of Last Farewell.

On nights with a moon Alek could keep an eye on her from the corner of the house. She was a small, insignificant spot surrounded by the dark sea and the starry night. When she turned to come back, he slipped under the blanket next to Ravnar again.

He only knew how she spent her days from what

he could see when he came home. The cabin was so clean and nice. The floor and the table had been scrubbed, and there was always a little bouquet of spring flowers that she must have sneaked out to pick by the stream. The cabin smelled as fresh as the grass on a summer day.

She had painted the sign for the inn, and Jona was impressed by the three lamb chops, the glass of wine, and the three oranges, one of them peeled and halfway split into segments so it opened like a flower. The tablecloth underneath was cream-colored lace, which revealed dark spots of the table beneath it. The sign hung above the door, and Jona had named the inn "Three of Each" and was happy that she had finally come up with a proper name.

Thala had used the rest of the paint to decorate the cabin's furniture. Orange and wine-red trim billowed along the backs of the chairs and around the little shelf Ravnar had built out of driftwood.

Ravnar's hand was slowly healing but it still hurt when he moved his fingers, and he could only bend and stretch them to a certain point.

"Those skippers are so greedy," he said. "They

exploit their crews. If only I had my own boat." He sighed while he sat, putting bait on the hooks on long lines, a job that otherwise was reserved for children and the old.

"There's a boat in Crow Cove," Alek reminded him.

"That little dinghy. Besides, I don't belong there." And then he said nothing for a long time.

But Thala didn't stay silent. She practiced conversing with Alek and he loved to hear her say: "Would you hand me the booter?" And "How it sturmed in the night!" The words tickled in his ears.

The pips in the little pot sent up three dark-green shoots. Thala nipped off the two smallest. The third unfolded a pair of leaves in the dusty spring sun. Thala took special care of the shoot with water and gull droppings, but she wasn't really happy.

One evening Alek took her little book and opened it to the last blank page. With the pencil he drew Crow Cove as best he could: the four houses and the stable, the stream that ran across the beach like the stream behind the cabin, the ridge that circled the

place, small sheep with stick legs and an eagle glid-
ing high on the page.

"Little town, very beautiful," said Thala, and
looked for a long time at the drawing.

"That's where I live," explained Alek.

"No, here," she objected.

"Just at the moment, otherwise I live there."

"There, you like best?"

Alek nodded.

"I like best, too."

"You can come with me." But Alek wasn't sure
that she understood him, and Ravnar growled: "What
on earth would she do in that crow corner?"

One night Alek didn't hear Thala get up. Instead he
woke to her tugging at his sleeve.

"Fire," she whispered.

Alek opened his eyes to a bottomless darkness. It
couldn't be. The fire had to be covered with ashes.

"On the beach," she continued, and he jumped up
and pulled on his pants, then eased the door open and
sneaked along the house wall to the corner of the
gable. Out there, at the end of the point, the same

place as last time, two bonfires flickered. He slipped inside again and woke up Ravnar.

"I'll go get my old skipper. He's a stupid swine, but he hates wreckers." He reached for his pants. "He says it ruins the trade here."

"Tell me where he lives, then I'll go get him! You'd better take care of Thala in case they show up here."

"You're right. Third house after the inn. Ask him to bring help!"

Ravnar struggled with his clothes in the dark; Alek took his jacket and hurried out.

There wasn't a single star in the sky. Once in a rare while the full moon appeared as a hazy shiny orb behind the racing clouds. The sea was in turmoil and the waves thundered against the beach. The wind came in gusts; suddenly it was still, then it tugged at him again.

He alternately climbed and crawled up the cliff, and he had almost reached the top when he heard someone coming. He let himself slide to the side of the path, and pressed his back against the cold rock, making himself as flat as a flounder.

The people who were passing were right next to him when his one foot slipped; rocks rattled into the deep, and his other foot began to lose its grip. Then he was grabbed by a huge claw and pulled up onto the path.

"Tell me, are you keeping watch?" said a voice, while the iron hand pinched harder and harder on his upper arm.

The voice was Sigge's.

"Let me go," cried Alek, and wriggled like a fish to get loose.

"Is that you, little Crow Cover?" Sigge loosened his grip but he didn't let go.

"Let me go! There are bonfires on the beach, and Ravnar and I can't handle the wreckers on our own."

"Come on!" called one of the others. "This time we won't let them succeed."

Alek could hear that it was the boatman who had snarled at him.

"How do I know that you're speaking the truth?" Sigge asked.

"Because someone is living with us who was on

the last ship they plundered. I hid her, so they wouldn't kill her."

Sigge released him. "There's no time to fetch more people. But go get Ravnar!"

Alek followed them.

A ship was coming. It danced across the waves with a tattered sail. The wind ripped the clouds from the moon, and its cold light plunged silver knives into the water.

Carefully Sigge and the other boatmen moved toward the bonfires. Alek and Ravnar hurried after them. The three men on the beach did not yet sense any danger.

"It's the same ones as last time," whispered Alek.

One tall and two shorter men armed with boat hooks.

"We have to put out those fires. They still have time to get her back on course if they use their oars," whispered Sigge.

"Why don't they use their eyes instead," growled one of the boatmen.

They divided the three men between them: Sigge

and the snarler would take the tall one, Ravnar and the three others the two shorter men. There was no one for Alek.

"You'll put out the fires," decided Sigge.

The ship had come closer. Stubbornly it hacked its way toward Last Farewell.

Then the action began. Sigge and his friends stormed out with raised clubs and the rest of the group at their heels. The three men on the beach tried to flee to the end of the point. Wood splintered against wood. The snarler screamed when a boat hook hit him in the chest.

The tall man had fought his way free and came rushing toward Alek, who was on his way to the bonfires. The moon lit up the man's face and Alek remembered that he had seen him in the harbor. The man did not notice him; he was running madly for a small dinghy pulled up at the water's edge.

Alek bent down and picked up a rock, heavy and round like a goose egg. He threw it with all his might and the man fell to his knees in front of the closest bonfire. A second later Sigge threw himself on top and forced the man's face into the stones.

The two young men, hands tied and with dragging feet, and no older than Tink, led the group. The snarler was supported by two other men. Alek picked up an even larger stone and began to choke the fire near him. Ravnar managed to put out the other bonfire.

"Row for your lives," screamed Sigge toward the ship, but the sail was already down and all oars were in the water.

When they reached the cabin, Thala stepped out from the corner of the white gable. She stared at the bound men; then she walked over to the tall man and stood in front of him.

Blood slowly dripped from his left temple down onto his shoulder. He clearly had no idea who she was or where she came from. She stood on tiptoes, looked straight into his eyes, and spit in his face; then she turned and walked back into the cabin.

11

The day had dawned by the time the three men were locked in a cellar with high windows. In the morning light, they were recognized as a local skipper and two young boatmen. Sigge arranged for a message to be sent to the magistrate in Eastern Harbor.

"Now she can move out," said Ravnar.

A cold wind came off the sea, but the sun warmed their backs. Ravnar and Alek sat down on some boxes in the empty harbor. All the boats had gone out at the first daylight, even though the sea was not yet calm. The gulls had followed the fishermen, but the jackdaws walked around in pairs, poking in tufts of grass and piles of seaweed.

"Why don't you wait until the magistrate has been here!" Alek leaned his whole body left and skipped a stone across the harbor's calm water.

"Good throw," said Ravnar.

"Only eight, I've done better."

"I meant last night."

"Oh, that," said Alek, and stuck his hands in his pockets.

They got up and the jackdaws rose in pairs, going their own ways.

"She can come with me to the inn. Then you'll have the cabin to yourself during the day."

Ravnar didn't answer, so it must be okay.

The heat arrived and the cod pulled away from the coast. The dried cod piled up in the small sheds along the water. People began to prepare their small garden plots for the new potatoes.

Thala accompanied Alek every day and Jona welcomed her. The young woman taught them how to cut old peeled potatoes into slices and cook them in fat, so they became crisp and light brown and you forgot all about their spongy past.

To Jona and Alek's astonishment, she poured wine into the pots, and she sometimes put a sprig of wormwood in the belly of a fish before roasting it over the embers.

In the evening they went home to Ravnar with these new dishes, which he wolfed down without many words. His hand was slowly getting better, and he sometimes spoke about going to sea again.

Thala did not get up in the night anymore, and she never went out onto Last Farewell, but Ravnar had begun to sleep uneasily and would wake up, get dressed, and leave the cabin. He was cold when he returned to lie beside Alek again.

When the magistrate arrived with his six men, everyone in town gathered at the harbor square. Jona closed the inn and went down with Alek and Thala. Ravnar was there already, and they joined him. Many people looked curiously at Thala.

"He brought her from Eastern Harbor," Alek heard one old woman whisper to another.

A small platform had been constructed out of wooden planks and boxes, and this was where the magistrate stood, dressed in black. He was wearing a broad-brimmed hat and his cape had been thrown back over his shoulders, so that his arms were free. He stood with his fists on his thighs and looked out over the square as people arrived from all sides. Above the gray beard, his large face glistened in the sun, and the silver buckle in his belt caught the rays and threw off dancing spots of light.

In front of him stood the three wreckers with heads bent and their hands bound behind their backs. The six men guarded them.

Thala caught sight of a face in the crowd and pointed it out to Alek. It was the man that had come down to the cabin and looked in the window.

"Who's the man with the curly hair?" Alek asked Ravnar.

"He's the one I asked to give you the message that I had gone to Eastern Harbor. Didn't he?"

"He tried," answered Alek.

The magistrate cleared his throat and everyone grew silent.

"Let us get to the point. Who brings these three men in front of the court?"

"I do."

Sigge stepped forward.

"And what do you believe is their crime?"

"I say the skipper's is murder and his boatmen's is complicity."

"All right. Now tell me what happened!"

Sigge did, and when he was done, the magistrate asked:

"What happened to the ship?"

"It turned around and disappeared."

"With everyone on board?"

Sigge nodded.

"Why do you call it murder then?"

"It has happened before. And the last time a ship went down, nine bodies drifted to shore. But a young woman who was on board was saved by a boy. It was the same boy who threw the stone that prevented the skipper from getting away."

"Let me see him!"

Alek's knees trembled as he made his way toward the platform. The magistrate put out a hand and pulled him up.

"What's your name, my boy?" he asked.

The skipper lifted his head and looked into his eyes without blinking even once.

"Alek."

If only his knees would stay still. They shook so that he felt the ripples all the way up in his brain, and all his thoughts were thrown about like driftwood. The continuous staring made the sweat erupt on his upper lip. He dried it off with the back of his hand.

"Speak!"

At first the words fell out of his mouth in random clumps. Then he caught sight of Ravnar in the crowd and locked his eyes on him.

Gradually the night took shape, the bonfires, the stranded ship. He could feel the dark fear and his fists gripped the stones in his pockets hard.

When he got to the killing blow, he became nauseous and felt like throwing up. His gaze wandered and met the skipper's, and he couldn't wrest it loose again. In his thoughts, he threw one of the stones from his pockets, so that it hit the murderer between the eyes. The skipper must have felt something because he lowered his eyes for the brief moment Alek needed to get free.

He found Ravnar and the thread of the story again and continued. When he finished, the magistrate called Thala forward. She positioned herself with her side to the wreckers so she wouldn't have to look at them.

"Where do you come from?" asked the magistrate. Thala answered.

"This will be difficult," said the magistrate, but Thala continued to speak and Alek suddenly realized that even though he understood her, the magistrate did not. Her accent was too thick.

"Wait," he yelled, and jumped down from the platform and ran, as fast as he could, past the inn, over the cliff, out to the cabin, where he tore Thala's little brown notebook down from the mantel and raced back with it.

Bending over with cramps, he handed the notebook to the magistrate. The big man took the thin book in his large hands and opened it. He looked for a long time at each page and when he got to the one with the blow, he pointed at the drawing of the man holding the oar and asked Thala:

"Who is that?"

She turned and pointed at the skipper. The magistrate closed the notebook and handed it to her, and then she and Alek were allowed to step down.

They hurried back to Ravnar and Jona. Eidi had made her way over to them as well.

"You managed that well," she said to Alek, and ruffled his hair, "but what was that about dress material for Myna?"

Alek laughed.

The magistrate asked the townspeople to choose a man and a woman who were well respected to conclude the trial with him.

"The innkeeper," suggested someone.

"No, someone from here," yelled someone else.

"Why?" Sigge asked. "The skipper is from this town. Does that make him better?"

"The innkeeper," several others now chimed in.

And Jona allowed herself to be chosen and was

proud. An elderly sailmaker was the other represen-
tative.

The three withdrew to the inn, while all the others remained standing in the square, waiting under
the cloudless sky.

12

Reffi and Eldrick."

The two young men stepped forward.

"You are brothers."

They nodded their heads.

"You come from the small hamlet behind the Gray Mountains called Sheep Grave."

That was true, too.

"You came here to earn a living as boatmen."

The magistrate didn't wait for an answer.

"You found yourselves a skipper who was bad in every way."

The crowd murmured its agreement.

"Your mistake was not that you followed his orders on board, but that you followed his orders on land."

An uneasiness spread across the square.

"You must leave town without your possessions, and you may never show yourselves here again. You will be escorted to the main road."

People began to comment on the judgment. Some were dissatisfied, others surprised; voices rose and fell, making a single note.

"Uwe," the magistrate said, and everyone grew silent. "You are a skipper with your own boat in Last Harbor."

No answer.

"You have committed wreckage with the help of a couple of boys; you have lured a crew to their death and killed a man in cold blood. There are witnesses."

He did not bow his head, nor move a muscle; he continued to stare.

"But what do you know about old Enver's death?"

Silence.

"Was it you who pushed him from the cliff path, because he had discovered what you were doing?"

"He fell," came the answer.

"You sound as certain as if you were there yourself."

The skipper's gaze began to wander. The magistrate cleared his throat.

"In the sea a bit north of the Hamlet there's a small island where a hermit once lived. The house is still there. The island is called the Claw. There you must spend a year of your life for each of the people for whose death we know you have been responsible."

"Nine years," whispered Alek.

"And all that you own will go to the young woman from whom you have stolen everything."

"What will she do with a boat?" whispered Ravnar.

"You will be sailed out to the island by one of my men and receive some tools so you can fish from the beach and tend the bit of ground that's there. Every midsummer a boat will come by so you can receive visitors and have the chance to trade. If anyone tries to help you to get away, they will share your fate.

"Everyone else who has collected driftwood or

other goods from the wrecked ship and has done so in good faith may keep it."

People stuck their heads together, and the volume in the square rose.

It grew silent again when the prisoners were led away. When the magistrate's broad black back disappeared from sight, the whole square moved. People made their way toward each other and went out to the boats or into town. Many set off in the direction of the inn.

Jona took Thala's arm and explained to her that the magistrate would come and pick her up at the inn to present her with her belongings. Uwe did not own the house he lived in, but all the furnishings would be hers and also the boat with lines and hooks and other gear.

"I have to go up to the store," said Eidi to Alek.

She gave him a hug and disappeared. He stood on his toes to see where Ravnar had gone when someone took his arm and he turned around. A pale young woman looked at him pleadingly.

"Here," she said, and stuck out a closed hand.

A heavy gold ring with a bloodred stone fell onto his open palm.

"I got it from him," she mumbled, and turned and ran away.

Alek put the ring into the pouch around his neck and hurried after the dark, longish hair he saw farther along in the crowd. Out of breath, he reached Ravnar's side.

"Well, now it's easier to understand why he always had to stop in at the Hamlet and Eastern Harbor," he said without looking at Alek. "And always on market days. But what she needed more was a place to live."

Jona lent Thala a shed for all her new things. There was a table and four chairs, a bench with blankets and pillows, and there were boxes and chests with fine porcelain packed in sawdust, silverware and sharp knives, barrels of wine and spices, lots of fabric, everyday clothes, fur, and valuable dresses, pearl necklaces and stolen conch shells.

Thala found the things from her own ship. It was only a small portion, but all the rest she wanted no part of, except for the boat and gear, which might be useful. The magistrate offered to have one of his men sell the rest at auction in the harbor square.

Eidi had invited Alek, Ravnar, and Thala to visit her after the auction. Everything had been sold, and the magistrate had gone to the inn himself to present Thala with a big sack of money. Jona had said that she and Alek should take the day off and go home, so they could enjoy Eidi's party.

Thala got out a big black skirt that was embroidered at the hem with a wavy golden design that looked like the one she had painted on the furniture. On top she wore a low-cut white blouse with the same trim in black and around her waist a thick gold scarf. A pair of long gold earrings dangled against her long white neck.

Alek and Ravnar walked down to the stream, pulled off their clothes, and scrubbed themselves with soap, rinsing off in the cold water. The sun was low in the sky, sending its last warm light across the shiny sea and giving their winter-pale bodies a tanned glow.

"You can't catch me!" yelled Alek, and raced across the round stones.

He had his arms spread out like a bird to keep his balance. Ravnar raced after him, grabbed him from behind, and gathered his wings. Alek flapped to get loose and Ravnar laughed and let go.

"You're it!"

The raven-black hair dangled against his back, so the water sprayed from it and sprinkled Alek in the face. Ravnar's legs were longer, but Alek's feet were faster. He threw his arms around his big brother's waist and held on tight. Ravnar bent down a little and pushed Alek up, so he rode on his back as he had done when he was little.

But Ravnar didn't carry him anywhere. He remained standing at the water's edge watching the sun disappear; then he carefully let Alek slide down, and together they returned to the bundles of clothes by the stream.

13

Eidi had invited several people that evening. Sigge was there, and the snarling man and a few more boat-men, the washerwoman's eldest daughter and her friend. The floor in the large parlor had been cleared, the chairs pulled to the side, and food set out by Eidi's cook on a long table against the wall. You could take a plate and fill it whenever you wanted.

"I've just learned a new musical game," said Eidi, and clapped her hands. "Sigge, will you play?"

Sigge pulled a small metal flute out of his pocket and played a few notes.

"The boys stand on one side and the girls on the other."

"There's not an equal number," objected the washerwoman's daughter.

"That doesn't matter. Not in this game."

Then Eidi walked over to Alek, took his hand, and pulled him onto the floor. She held his hand while she sang and Sigge accompanied her:

> *"I went to town to find a sweetheart,*
> *but who it should be,*
> *that was the hard part.*
> *Few were rich,*
> *Many were poor.*
> *Some were serious,*
> *And still more ridiculous,*
> *Most were too young,*
> *Others too doddering,*
> *A few too ugly, a very few a bit more lucky."*

She let go of Alek's hand.

> *"To choose someone new,*
> *Say goodbye to the old one.*

If you don't get chosen,
Then choose yourself.
Turn your back on yesterday . . ."

"Turn your back to me!" she whispered to Alek, and they turned their backs on each other.

"And say hello to today,
And then choose him and her
That you most want to have!"

"Then you choose someone!" she said to Alek, "and I will, too. But we're not allowed to see who the other person chooses, so you're not allowed to turn around!"

Thala stood dark and golden between the two blond women. Her eyes shone, and she smiled at him. He walked over and stood in front of her.

"Did you choose?" asked Eidi.

"Yes."

"Then lead her onto the floor!"

"Now you may think,
You're made for each other,

But just wait to see,
Who'll get each other."

Thala and Ravnar were left in the middle of the floor, while Alek and Eidi each backed into their rows.

Ravnar's water-combed hair was gathered in a leather cord at his nape, his white linen shirt was gray with wash and wear. He drooped a bit, looking at the ground.

One of the girls giggled, and the snarling man laughed briefly. Ravnar straightened up and looked at Thala. Then it became completely still, while the night breathed through the open window and made the lights quiver.

"You have to kiss each other!" said Eidi.

Thala turned around and looked at her. Then she looked at Ravnar with a smile and a moment later she loosened the golden scarf tied around her waist and placed it in front of her mouth and kissed him gently through the shiny fabric. He stood unmoving and let it happen.

"I went to town to find a sweetheart . . ."

Eidi began again, while Sigge's flute raced after and caught up with her.

Ravnar turned on his heel and left the parlor. Thala remained standing with the scarf dragging on the floor. Her smile was gone. Eidi continued to sing while she went over and pulled the snarling man onto the floor so the game could continue.

Ravnar sat like a dark shadow in front of a small fire. His bent back faced the door and he didn't lift his head until they had come all the way over to the table. The air was heavy with the scent of tobacco smoke and the smell of tar that must have stuck to the wood. He sat, rubbing his scarred hand, bending and stretching his fingers and finally making a fist with them before he placed his hand heavily on the table.

"I want to row the boat to Crow Cove—together with you two," he said.

Alek pulled a chair over to the table and sat down. Thala leaned on the edge of the alcove.

"Maybe we'll be lucky and get a day with a calm northern wind, so we can set the sail."

He opened his hand and reached for his pipe. He scratched the inside clean and filled it again. The spicy blue smoke mixed with the sour yellowish haze that hung in the air.

Alek walked over and threw open the door. The stars were grains of sand on the night's dark cloth; a bird's fine whistling could be heard over the water.

"And then what?" he asked out into the air.

"Then you'll have a good boat in Crow Cove and I'll have my cabin to myself."

Alek made fists of his hands while his toes began to prick. Something spread all the way from down at the underside of his toenails and pressed its way up through his legs and thighs and out through his entire body. His throat was tight with the great pressure from below, and his cheeks burned. Then his feet loosened and he raced back in and threw himself at Ravnar.

It had to come out, that violent, angry red. It streamed through his arms and pounded his fists against Ravnar's shoulders and back. It grabbed the black, smooth hair and tugged at it. And when Ravnar seized his wrists, it continued to spit and kick to make a place for itself. It had no words, it was without thought, it just wanted.

Then the crying came racing with hollow hiccups. He wanted to stop it, to force it back, but it would not be stopped, it had to come up and out.

"What's the matter, you crazy kid?"

Alek gasped a mouthful of air.

"You . . . you're so dark," he hacked. "You leave while the game is good. You . . ." And it took him a while to control his voice: "You won't have fun."

Ravnar shrugged uneasily.

"You're like an old man," screamed Alek shrilly. "You're not Ravnar at all anymore."

Ravnar got up and took his jacket and left the house. The sound of gravel crunching under his feet quickly grew fainter. Thala remained unmoving on the edge of the alcove. Alek went outside and sat down with his back to the brick gable.

A line of white foam separated the black water from the dark beach, and only the teeming stars revealed where the sea ended and the sky began.

There was a roar far away from over the sea, and then it was silent.

Alek shivered and continued to sit, waiting. At first he froze but after a while he no longer felt the cold. When Ravnar finally returned, the sky to the east had taken on a delicate pink color in the crack between night and day.

14

Now everyone in town knows my name," said Jona with satisfaction, and stuck a wooden spoon out in front of her.

All the wooden implements had been covered in a paste of pipe clay overnight and now appeared bright white.

Alek sat, scraping a bucketful of the most delicate, small new potatoes. The peel was as thin as the membrane on the inside of an eggshell.

"That was the first thing the magistrate wanted to know: my name."

Her ruddy cheeks glowed, as they had done every time she talked about it.

"Who would have thought it, when I ran away with the innkeeper from Last Harbor?"

"Ran away?"

"Oh, yes."

She dropped a spoon that she wasn't satisfied with back into the basin.

"For many years I traveled around with a drunkard. Burd was his name."

She dried her hands on her apron and pushed her hair away from her forehead.

"I haven't seen him for several years. I wonder what happened to him."

"He's buried in Crow Cove," Alek told her.

"He is? Well, he had to come to an end somewhere."

She plunged her hands into the basin again.

"Well, at a certain point we had no more money or food or drink, and then he sold his horse to the innkeeper. Afterward they drank on it and Burd went under the table. Though that did not happen often.

"That's when the innkeeper asked if I wouldn't

rather stay with him. And I was tired of the wet life and the dry beatings, and I got to be sweet on him, too. When he died, I inherited the inn. So now I'm here and I'm planning to stay."

"We are going home to Crow Cove."

"Oh, and I've been happy to have you here—and her as well. But Ravnar, he's coming back, isn't he?"

Yes, Ravnar was coming back. Alek flung a potato into the water so that it splashed on all sides.

The sun had been shining since they got up. The wind was fresh and from the north. The cool morning air had warmed by the time Ravnar locked the little cabin.

Alek threw his skin satchel over his shoulder. There was a tinkling sound from the little pouch he carried around his neck. That was all he had to carry; Jona had gotten back her pails and Eidi her blankets.

Up on the cliff, he turned around. The two little windows on either side of the door caught the sunlight and sent it into his face and waved him on.

Jona came out of the inn with a packed lunch for them. The jackdaws flew up onto the roof and stood in the air with flapping wings before they landed again. The gulls scolded a cat that ran across the harbor square with a kitten in its mouth. The kitten whimpered so that you could look straight into its pink mouth. Down by the boat Sigge and Eidi were waiting.

"Are you sure you can manage on your own?" Sigge asked Ravnar. "It's a makeshift crew you've chosen and you've got no first mate."

"It'll be fine," said Ravnar. "The wind is with us."

It was. When they had rounded Last Farewell, they could set the sail and let themselves be led away from the black-and-white-checked town with the black and white birds that circled in and out of the chimney smoke.

The little cabin appeared and the view of Last Harbor disappeared. The cabin's white gable turned its back on them while the little windows stared the other way, toward town. The cabin was the last house before Crow Cove.

The sun was high in the sky when they opened their packed lunch.

"Three of each. Love, Jona," it said on a little note she had placed inside.

Three hard-boiled eggs, three oat buns, and three of each of everything else. They had a jug of water from the stream, and when they had drunk, Thala gave the little orange tree in the bottom of the boat a splash of water.

Rocky cliffs, grassy slopes, inlets, streams, stony beaches, and reefs alternated down along the coast. A flock of gulls followed a school of fish, and high above their heads an eagle circled in large, soft arcs.

"Look," shouted Thala, when the seals that had been lying and sunning themselves slid into the sea.

The boat smelled of tar and rope. Alek leaned back and let his gaze follow the ragged and undulating line that the hills drew against the sky. The day was drawing to a close, the light had gotten warmer, the air cooler. The boat turned a bit in toward land, and Alek could tell by the water's whirls that there must be a reef right below the surface. Myna's house appeared, a little white block against the green hillside behind it. He turned and looked at Ravnar.

He must have sailed here before. Often. This

close to Crow Cove. Perhaps it was here that he had turned around every time or perhaps he had sailed a bit farther so that Rossan's gable had peeked out up along the stream. So that he had also seen the potato house, the stable, and Frid and Foula's house. And his little brother on the beach.

Ravnar's face revealed nothing.

In the cove, they had to get out the oars. Glennie came panting from up at the bridge and figures appeared in the landscape.

Frid was the first to reach the beach. He waded out with Glennie barking around his legs and helped pull the heavy boat onto shore.

Then he turned to Thala and gave her his hand. The water poured from the bottom of her long skirt and her cheeks were red with effort.

"What a pretty girl you've brought along."

He smiled at Ravnar's unmoving face.

"This is Thala," Alek butted in. "And she's with us both."

Glennie raced up the path to meet Myna. Myna's eyes shone happy and blue on either side of her bent nose. She smiled at Ravnar and hugged Alek.

"Hello to you, little kid."

She gave him a squeeze, let go of him, and turned to Ravnar.

He nodded at her and then began to walk quickly in the opposite direction of all the others who were on their way down to join them.

15

The next day Ravnar walked up the path that ran by Myna's house, farther along the stream and then up over the hilltop. Alek and Frid kept him company. At the top they stopped and turned around and looked out across the cove.

The little white houses shone in the sun, and the fields, framed by the light-gray stone walls, looked like large squares with green stripes. White sheets waved at them from the clothesline as did a gold scarf in a hand a bit farther on.

"It's Thala," said Alek.

She came running up the path.

"I didn't get to properly say goodbye," Ravnar admitted, and went to meet her.

Alek could see that he held her around the shoulders and bent down toward her. They stood like that for a while before he let her go and came up again. This time he didn't stop. Frid hurried after him and gave him his hand.

"I'll say goodbye here," he said. "It was good to see you again."

"Likewise," said Ravnar, and hurried on.

Alek ran after him. When he was right behind him, he reached for his belt.

"What are you doing?"

"Holding on."

Ravnar tried to reach him but Alek wriggled from side to side and avoided his hands.

"Let me go!"

Ravnar got a grip on his wrist.

"Not before you say you'll come again."

Ravnar tried to pull his hand away, but Alek swallowed the pain and clung on even tighter to the narrow strip of leather.

"Let me go now!"

"When I know when you are coming back."

Ravnar turned around with such power that Alek was flung into the cliff wall. The belt snapped and flew off the pants. Alek still had it in his hand when Ravnar helped him up. He let go of it and made fists.

"Crazy kid," said Ravnar, and pulled him close and threw his arms around him.

And Alek let himself be embraced and leaned his forehead against Ravnar's coarse, sun-warmed shirt in exhaustion.

"I'll come at midwinter."

Ravnar grabbed Alek's hair and pulled his head back and looked into his eyes.

"I promise you."

But now it was summer, rip-roaring summer, with white days and the smell of hay.

Thala's boat was large enough for three, so Alek could start fishing with Tink and Kotka, and every time they went out they came home with a full load.

The cow gave milk, and the cream was thick and

the butter smooth and yellow. Little red strawberries shone on the hillsides, ripe for picking.

The sunshine lured out new smells. Alek thought the skin on his arms smelled of fresh-baked bread, and even the bare cliffs took on a new, unfamiliar scent of warm stones.

All the animals were out; only the hens used the stable to find hiding places for their eggs. Outside, the manure pile spewed out black clouds of flies, and horseflies bit into your browned skin and made the horses flick their tails.

In the kitchen garden, the onions lay in long rows, drying in the sun, before Thala and Foula braided them into garlands that were hung up in the attic along with bunches of dried herbs. The potato knobs spilled out of the black dirt when you turned it. Everything was bounteous.

Only Thala wasn't really happy. Over and over her gaze sought the path where Ravnar had disappeared.

"He's coming at midwinter," said Alek.

But Thala didn't know what midwinter was.

*   *   *

Then it was harvest time, and Eidi came sailing with boat and boatmen to trade goods and bring Crow Cove's excess to the big fall market in Last Harbor. She hadn't seen much of Ravnar. He was sailing for a new skipper now and seldom showed himself in town. She thought his hand was as good as it was going to get.

Before she left she promised Foula that she and Sigge would be in Crow Cove for Dark Night.

The wild geese made their way south, and Myna's flock of geese craned their necks at them and flapped their clipped wings. Alek laid his head back and followed the wedge of birds with his eyes until it disappeared behind the roof.

Glennie put her front paws on the ground, so that her wagging tail was the highest point of her, and then she jumped up and danced around him and stuck her tail into the air again. Up on her legs, a bit up the path, back and wagging her tail; come on, oh, come on!

Alek laughed and followed her.

The morning was cool and clear, and the cold water

from the stream washed the last thick sleep away while Glennie ran off the night's stiffness. The sun shone straight into his face when he reached the hillcrest.

Glennie chased a guinea hen that flew, harvest-heavy, out over the heather. The landscape flamed in gold and orange. Little blackberries stained hands and lips and crunched bittersweet between the teeth.

The path snaked up and down and in and out, and the stream flashed silver between the hills. The black bog holes lay like silent graves in the midst of the vivid life.

Glennie stood stock-still over a small field mouse and managed to hit it with her paw and place the little warm body before Alek's feet. He pushed it out to the side and Glennie pounced on the animal one more time and swallowed it in a single mouthful. Alek turned his head away and caught sight of a figure that sketched a black shadow against the shining, pale-blue sky.

"Who's that?" he asked Glennie, pointing. She followed his hand and raced along with the same speed she otherwise used only when the summer-wild male lambs needed to be rounded up.

It was Ravnar. He was both tired and happy when he caught sight of Alek. He had walked all night because it had been quiet and starry and the moon had been full.

Alek danced around him just like a dog and threw little punches at him.

"What are you doing here? You weren't going to come until midwinter. Go ahead and turn around." He laughed happily.

Punch, punch. Then he let his fists fall. Ravnar threw his arm across Alek's shoulders, and they walked on. Up there on the hills they could make out the sea far away, the water and the light shining against each other and intensifying their blue.

"It's no fun being alone when you've gotten used to better," said Ravnar.

He let go of Alek and let him lead the way down the steep path.

Alek picked up the split oar and carried it over to the pile of driftwood. All along the coast lay light-gray piles. All the pieces of wood that in the course of the year had been tossed farther up onto land so that the waves would not take them back were now gathered together to be ferried home to Crow Cove.

"There's less than usual, and we are more," said Myna.

"Rossan says that we have to start digging peat."

"Yes, we might need to do that."

Myna whistled for Glennie, who came racing after them. A pair of ducks took flight a bit farther on and raced, frightened, out over the water.

"That one we'll have to pick up together."

Alek walked over to her and grabbed the other end of the plank. They carried it a good way up onto land and then they threw all the other pieces they found nearby on top.

The air was heavy with moisture and made the cliffs black and slippery. The sea and the sky blended together in a dusk-gray mist.

"We're turning around now," said Myna, and pulled her shawl up around her head.

Alek threw the last stick down and poked his ice-cold hands into his clammy pockets. A flock of terns raced by on their flight from the darkness and cold.

"Wood fire smells the best anyway," said Myna, and hid her hands under the half-wet shawl.

Alek bent down over a rounded board from a barrel lid and threw it on the next pile they passed. A pair of silver-gray branches slid to the sides and landed on the ground. Myna picked them up and returned them to the pile before they continued.

"And Ravnar came home."

Alek nodded. In the distance a sheep bleated for its flock.

"He was my friend once." She cleared her throat. "And maybe he can become so again."

When they reached Crow Cove, Myna went home and Alek continued across the bridge toward the potato house. Tink had lived in one end for a long time, and they had stored potatoes in the other. But now Ravnar and Tink and Frid had expanded the stable with a storage room, so that there was room for Ravnar in the house.

Alek stepped into the freshly whitewashed parlor. Ravnar and Frid each sat in a chair with their legs stretched out toward the warmth. Alek hung his wet jacket on a nail and looked around for a third chair, but there was none.

"You can sit here," Frid suggested, and closed his legs and patted his thigh.

Alek hesitantly settled down, carefully using Frid's arm as a backrest.

The flame from a single candle was reflected in the glass in the little window that faced the hills. The light from the fire in the hearth billowed golden across the snow-white walls while the smoke from Ravnar's pipe mellowed the clammy smell of lime.

Alek's cold fingers began to prickle, and the warmth spread slowly through his body. The fire made small, crackling noises, Ravnar puffed on his pipe, and the rain hit the window and startled the little light.

Alek let his head sink onto Frid's shoulder and allowed his late afternoon sleepiness to take over. Boards and branches, planks and barrel lids made patterns behind his closed lids. Silver-gray wood, silk-smooth wood, washed free of all unnecessary colors, kindling and timber and sea-chest wood from ships that would never sail again.

The door in the hallway opened, and Alek opened his eyes and hurriedly stood up.

Cam poked his head in.

"Are you coming over for dinner?"

They were.

16

Winter was upon them with violent storms and still, rain-heavy weather. The woolly daylight came slowly and faded quickly again. Foula's spinning wheel spun the days together in an even thread.

The wilted grass became dark with water, and the dried seaweed on the beach swelled to black, solid heaps. The driftwood lay in piles in the rain. Only the best pieces, which would be used for gates and hatches, had been stored in the stable.

The cow chewed the sweet-smelling hay, which offered winter shelter for the mice that had been babies that summer. The horses moved their heavy heads and finally accepted the narrow quarters. Everyone slept late and went to bed early.

Midwinter was near.

Cam lay sleeping with his round cheek pressed flat, so that his lower eye was forced into a narrow slit. His mouth was open and a thin thread of spittle had found its way from mouth to pillow.

Alek had lain the same way last year. But this year he would not give in. He stared with dry, tired eyes at the little light that would continue burning for a long time yet.

Eidi and Sigge had sung and played all the songs they knew, and all the stories had been told. In the silence Thala got up and rustled around in the corner. Then she came over to Alek and placed something in his lap. Something white and soft.

In the low light he could make out that it was a shirt, with light-blue stars embroidered on the yoke and white mother-of-pearl buttons.

He pulled off his old worn shirt and pulled the new one over his head. It smelled sun-warm and spicy and was a little too long in the sleeves, but he just rolled them up.

Then he turned to thank her but she had gone over to Ravnar and had given him a shirt of shiny dark-blue silk with silver-gray stars.

Frid put a bit more kindling on the fire so they could admire the presents. The flames created a half circle of light out into the room. The blue fabric gave Ravnar's hair a green metallic sheen like a bird feather and his skin shone yellow like old ivory.

"You look handsome, too," said Myna, and Alek knew that Ravnar was the most handsome.

The wind had died down and a faint light spread outside the windows. The flame in the skull sputtered, but it fought for its life. Finally you couldn't see it anymore in the daylight that came streaming in. Then it gave up and let the wick drown in the last bit of wax.

Frid walked over and opened the door. The fresh, cool morning air chased the last shadows from Dark Night. It was Light Morning, and everyone went outside. Only Ravnar and Alek remained standing in the doorway.

"If only I had had a gift for her as well," exclaimed Ravnar, pushing his hands into his pockets and gazing at Thala, who was on her way down to the beach.

There the sun's rays had reached land while the rest of the cove still lay in shadow. A memory appeared in Alek's mind. Something pale and sad, something bloodred and heavy.

"I have a present," he told Ravnar, and raced across the bridge and into his room.

Where was it, his little skin pouch? He looked through all his pockets and found it at last hanging on a leather cord on the hook beneath his oldest pants.

It was still there, the gold ring with the bloodred stone that he had gotten from the girl in the harbor square and had then totally forgotten.

He pressed the ring into his fist, ran back to Ravnar, and let it drop into his hand.

"Where did you get that?"

Alek told him.

"Perhaps it's a sad present."

"I don't have anything else," said Alek.

"I don't either," said Ravnar, sticking the ring in his pocket and setting off after Thala.

"Come on, Glennie!" Alek called, and the dog came leaping.

Together they walked across the bridge and by Myna's house, where she and Kotka were probably already sleeping in each other's arms.

The sun had reached the hill behind the house, and Alek crawled up into the wet, wilted grass. From here he could look out over all of Crow Cove. The houses still lay in shadow, but the sun hit the smoke from the chimneys, and out at the water's edge the stream spread its silver fan toward the glittering sea. Thala and Ravnar had melted together into a little dark spot that was moving away from him.

"Come on, Glennie!" he yelled, but the old dog had run back and lain down in her place in front of the door.

So he continued over the hill and down onto the beach. The sea was as mild as breath and blue as a gaze. Alek found a small flat stone and skipped it across the shiny surface.

He went on and found another and another.

Finally he reached the place where they had found his little horse, a very long time ago. Back then he had been so little that he was still called Doup and couldn't stay awake on Dark Night.

There was nothing left. The hard storms had long ago moved all the bones and washed the beach clean.

He sat down on a stone close by. He was at once dizzy with exhaustion and wide awake. His gaze slid out to sea, out over the edge of the world, all the way to nothing.

And in one glimpse he understood what he saw. The waves rise to lie down again. Ships are built and ships are lost. Small horses live and small horses die. You are born and you disappear in an unending chain.

And his time on earth was right here, right now, in the clear morning where his life tied the world together in an eternal moment.